The Great Grey Ghost of Old Spook Lane

Book, Music, and Lyrics by Anne Phillips

Baker's Plays
7611 Sunset Blvd.
Los Angeles, CA 90042
bakersplays.com

RENTAL MATERIALS

An orchestration consisting of **Piano/Vocal Score** and **Sound Effects CD** will be loaned two months prior to the production ONLY on the receipt of the Licensing Fee quoted for all performances, the rental fee and a refundable deposit.

Please contact Samuel French for perusal of the music materials as well as a performance license application.

CHARACTERS

ROGER/ROBIN - the new kid in school (may be played by either a boy or girl)

THE GANG:

SCOTT

GREG

JIMMY

BRIAN

JENNIFER

LAURIE

PAM

JO ANN

THE GREAT GREY GHOST - older child with grey hair and a long grey beard

A fun project for the group is to make the props for the Ghostly Repast: evil eye soup, phantom pie, etc.

SONGS

1. OVERTURE
2. SCHOOL FOOD
3. ALL IN A BRAND NEW DAY
4. THE HOUSE ON OLD SPOOK LANE
5. TO MAKE THEM LIKE ME
6. MY SIMPLE WAY OF LIVING
7. THERE'S NO SUCH THING AS HAUNTED
8. A GHOSTLY REPAST
9. TO MAKE THEM LIKE ME - reprise

SCENES AND MUSICAL NUMBERS

SCENE 1 – Lunchtime in the school cafeteria
  SCHOOL FOOD – The gang
  ALL IN A BRAND NEW DAY – Roger
  THE HOUSE ON OLD SPOOK LANE – The gang
  TO MAKE THEM LIKE ME – Roger

SCENE 2 – Outside the Ghost's house that night

SCENE 3 – Same night. Inside the Ghost's house
  MY SIMPLE WAY OF LIVIN' - The Ghost
  TO MAKE THEM LIKE ME (reprise) - The Ghost

SCENE 4 – Later the same night. Inside the Ghost's house
  THERE'S NO SUCH THING AS HAUNTED - The gang

SCENE 5 – The next night. Inside the Ghost's house
  A GHOSTLY REPAST – The Ghost

SCENE 6 – The next day. Lunchtime in the school cafeteria

SCENE 7 – That afternoon. The Ghost's front door

CURTAIN CALLS
  TO MAKE THEM LIKE ME (reprise)

SCENE 1

(The action takes place in the cafeteria of the school at lunch time. The kids in the "gang" enter carrying their books.)

SCOTT. Boy, that was a bummer of a test Mrs. Miller gave us in math this morning. Fractions! Who needs fractions! And she didn't even tell us we were going to have a test!

LAURIE. Sure she did, Scott. Last Friday. She said, "Monday morning we are going to have a test on fractions. Study pages 67 to 72!" Where were you?

JENNIFER. Gazing out the window thinking about new accessories for his dirt bike, I bet.

(They push two tables together, plop their books down on them and head for the food counter.)

SCOTT. Yuk - look what they got for lunch today!

JIMMY. Dog food smells better than this stuff!

JENNIFER. Seventy-five cents for this junk - boy!

BRIAN. I think I'll tell my mom to start making me sandwiches again!

(One by one, they pick up trays and start putting plates of food on them.)

LAURIE. Oooh - look at that green runny stuff - I bet it's creamed spinach again.

JO ANN. Who could stand to eat this junk every day?

PAM. Sometimes it's not so bad - like when we have spaghetti and garlic bread.

GREG. My dad says having bread with spaghetti is like having water with watermelon.

JO ANN. Aaggh - I think I found a bug in my corn!

JIMMY. That's better than finding half a bug! HA HA HA!

JENNIFER. My sister says at the high school lunch room you have your choice of three different things for lunch. And if you don't like any of them you can always have a hamburger. Wow - high school. *(She stares off dreamily.)*

BRIAN. Yeah - the food there's gotta be better than this!

SONG - SCHOOL FOOD

SCHOOL FOOD, SCHOOL FOOD
IF YOU HAD TO EAT IT, YOU'D COME UNGLUED!
SCHOOL FOOD, SCHOOL FOOD
IT SURE DOESN'T PUT YOU IN AN EATING MOOD.

 HEY WHAT'S THAT FUNNY THING IN YOUR NOODLES?
I SEE A HEAD
I SEE TWO EYES
THIS ICKY STUFF'S NOT FIT FOR MY POODLE
I THINK IT'S JUST A BUNCH OF WORMS IN DISGUISE

SCHOOL FOOD, SCHOOL FOOD
IF YOU HAD TO EAT IT, YOU'D COME UNGLUED!
SCHOOL FOOD, SCHOOL FOOD
IT SURE DOESN'T PUT YOU IN AN EATING MOOD.

IT SAYS HERE "MONDAY LUNCH WILL BE BEEFSTEAK"
CAN'T CUT IT WITH A HATCHET
OH, WHAT A SHAME
IF YOU ATE THAT BOY, YOU'D GET A STOMACH ACHE
HEY, THAT'S THE OLD SHOE
I LOST AT THE GAME

SCHOOL FOOD, SCHOOL FOOD
IF YOU HAD TO EAT IT, YOU'D COME UNGLUED!
SCHOOL FOOD, SCHOOL FOOD
IT SURE DOESN'T PUT YOU IN AN EATING MOOD.

DO YOU REMEMBER THAT WEIRD CHICKEN CHOW MEIN?
I SWEAR IT WAS MOVING
YOU THINK IT WAS TAME?
AND CARDBOARD PIZZA - THAT'S HARD TO EXPLAIN
TO CAMOUFLAGE THE TASTE
IS THEIR CLAIM TO FAME

SCHOOL FOOD, SCHOOL FOOD
IF YOU HAD TO EAT IT, YOU'D COME UNGLUED!
SCHOOL FOOD, SCHOOL FOOD
IT SURE DOESN'T PUT YOU IN AN EATING MOOD.

(At the end of the song, they all sit down at the table and begin to eat.)

GREG. Hey Jimmy, I'll trade ya the rest of my corn for half of your Jell-o.

JIMMY. OK.

PAM. *(holding up ketchup bottle)* Anybody want ketchup?

*(**SCOTT** grabs bottle and begins pounding the bottom over **JENNIFER**'s plate)*

SCOTT. *(sings)* Anticipation...

JENNIFER. Look out! You'll get it all over everything!

SCOTT. So? It'll taste better!

*(**ROGER** enters. He looks unsurely at the gang's table then heads for an empty one. He sits down and begins to eat. He puts his books down and goes to the food counter.)*

JIMMY. Hey, how about that new kid we got in class this morning?

SCOTT. What a weirdo!

(He makes a face crossing his eyes and pulling out his ears.)

LAURIE. What d'ya expect? Someone said he moved here from Granville. You know what jerks those kids from Granville are!

BRIAN. Did you see that dumb hat he was wearing?

PAM. And a book bag - blah!

*(**ROGER** sits down and begins to eat. They realize he is at the other table nudge each other.)*

GREG. What a nerd.

SCOTT. Pretend you don't see him.

*(**ROGER** picks at his food and begins to sing.)*

SONG - ALL IN A BRAND NEW DAY

ROGER.
>I WOKE UP IN A BRAND NEW BED
>IN A ROOM I DIDN'T KNOW
>I LOOKED AT MYSELF WITH A BRAND NEW SMILE
>AND HAD A DIFFERENT PLACE TO GO
>
>I WALKED ALONG A BRAND NEW STREET
>PAST AN UNFAMILIAR STORE
>AND I SAID NOT A WORD TO THE PEOPLE I SAW
>THAT I'D NEVER SEEN BEFORE
>
>BUT IT'S ALL IN A BRAND NEW DAY FOR ME
>ONE I'VE NEVER LIVED BEFORE
>I'M LIVIN' IN A BRAND NEW WAY FOR ME
>AND I'M SURE I'LL LIKE IT MORE
>
>I OPENED UP A BRAND NEW DOOR
>AND WALKED DOWN A BRAND NEW HALL
>I HEARD ALL THE LAUGHTER FROM EVERY ROOM
>AND THE NAMES I'D LEARN TO CALL
>
>I SAT DOWN IN A BRAND NEW CHAIR
>NEXT TO KIDS I DIDN'T KNOW
>AND THOUGH NOBODY CAME AND SHOOK MY HAND
>I'M SURE THEY THOUGHT "HELLO"
>
>BUT IT'S ALL IN A BRAND NEW DAY FOR ME
>ONE I'VE NEVER LIVED BEFORE
>I'M LIVIN' IN A BRAND NEW WAY FOR ME
>AND I'M SURE, YES, I'M SURE I'LL LIKE IT MORE

PAM. Who stuck their finger in my pudding?

LAURIE. I didn't think you liked pudding!

PAM. Sure I do – It's just that gross skin on top I can't stand. But I dig all the good stuff out from underneath it.

JENNIFER. Hey, JoAnn, you look like you're putting on weight.

JOANN. Sure, I am. Garbage is fattening.

BRIAN. (*tasting container of milk*) Aaggh - warm milk again.

>(*The kids continue eating.* **SCOTT** *looks over at the table where* **ROGER** *is eating alone. He ponders a moment then says...*)

SCOTT. Hey, kid…you wanna come over and sit with us?

ROGER. Yeah…OK.

> (**ROGER** *comes over to the table carrying his tray. The* **KIDS** *make room for him.*)

SCOTT. What'd you say your name was?

ROGER. Roger.

SCOTT. Roger what?

ROGER. Roger Brightbill.

JIMMY. Brightbill - ya sure it's not dumbbell?

> (*Everybody laughs.*)

BRIAN. When did ya move here?

ROGER. We just moved in last Saturday.

JIMMY. Where do you live?

ROGER. On Ivy Road.

SCOTT. Ivy Road! - You mean you live on old Spook Lane?!

JIMMY. That's what everybody around here calls Ivy Road 'cause of the haunted house.

SCOTT. Do you live near the haunted house, Rog?

ROGER. I don't know - where's the haunted house?

JIMMY. Number 17 Ivy Road.

ROGER. Our house is Number 19.

SCOTT. WOW! - You live right next door to the haunted house. Wow, I wouldn't want to live there!

JIMMY. Ya hear any weird sounds coming from it, Rog?

ROGER. Gee - I didn't even know it was haunted - I mean it's back there behind all those trees 'n everything. Is it really – h-h-haunted?

SCOTT. Is it ever!

SONG - THE HOUSE ON OLD SPOOK LANE

ALL EXCEPT ROGER.
> BEHIND THE TREES AND HEDGES HIGH
> THERE IS A GHOST DOMAIN
> IT'S OLD AND WORN AND TUMBLE-DOWN
> IT'S THE HOUSE ON OLD SPOOK LANE

UPON THE DOORSTEP I HAVE SEEN
A DARK AND BLOODY STAIN
AND AWFUL THINGS GO ON IN THERE
IN THE HOUSE ON OLD SPOOK LANE

OOOOOOOOOOO
THE HOUSE ON OLD SPOOK LANE
OOOOOOOOOOO
THE HOUSE ON OLD SPOOK LANE

THE COBWEBS THERE HANG THICK AND LOW
ACROSS EACH WINDOW PANE
AND THE WIND GOES HOWLING THROUGH THE EAVES
IN THE HOUSE ON OLD SPOOK LANE

THE MAN WHO LIVED THERE YEARS AGO
THEY SAY WAS QUITE INSANE
AND HIS CRAZY LAUGHTER ECHOS STILL
IN THE HOUSE ON OLD SPOOK LANE

OOOOOOOOOOO
THE HOUSE ON OLD SPOOK LANE
OOOOOOOOOOO
THE HOUSE ON OLD SPOOK LANE

HE HAD A STRANGE AND GRUESOME PET
WITH A LONG AND POINTED FANG
AND HE SLITHERED UP AND DOWN THE STEPS
OF THE HOUSE ON OLD SPOOK LANE

AND EVERY NIGHT THE NEIGHBORS HEAR
THE RATTLING OF CHAINS
IF THERE EVER WAS A HAUNTED HOUSE
IT'S THE HOUSE ON OLD SPOOK LANE

OOOOOOOOOOO
THE HOUSE ON OLD SPOOK LANE
OOOOOOOOOOO
THE HOUSE ON OLD SPOOK LANE

SCOTT. Boy - I remember one time when I was in there I heard…

ROGER. Ya, ya mean you really went in the haunted house?

SCOTT. *(boastfully)* Sure, we've all been in it. Every kid around here's been in it - unless he's chicken. But we've all been in it haven't we?

GANG. Yeah - sure.

SCOTT. Anyway, when I was in it I heard these spooky footsteps coming up from the cellar plop - plop - plop- Boy, did I get out fast!

JENNIFER. Yeah, when I was in it I heard this funny laugh and then something came running across the floor shouting, "BOGGIE boogie BOOGIE boogie."

ROGER. What was it?

JENNIFER. I don't know, it was too dark to tell.

ROGER. D-D-Dark! Ya mean you went in at night?!!

SCOTT. Sure! - Night time's the only time to go into a haunted house - unless, of course, you're chicken.

ROGER. H-how do you get in?

SCOTT. Oh, that's easy! There's this one window in the living room that doesn't have a lock on it. But, you gotta be careful because there's a big vase right in front of it and sometimes when you push the window up the vase falls over.

GREG. Yeah - I must have knocked that vase down a dozen times - must be plastic cause it never breaks. And the next time you go back - there it is standing right in front of the window again. Weird!

SCOTT. Well, how 'bout it, Rog? Want to go into the haunted house tonight? It's easy for you I mean you live right next door 'n everything.

ROGER. I-I think it's supposed to rain tonight, isn't it?

SCOTT. Great, that's even better! That's really the time to go into a haunted house on a rainy night!

(turns to gang)

Can you guys all come? Jennifer?

JENNIFER. Sure, I'll just tell my parents I'm going over to your house Laurie, to do some homework. OK?

LAURIE. OK.

SCOTT. Pam? Jimmy?

GANG. You bet. Sure.

SCOTT. OK, then. Let's all meet there about seven. OK with you, Rog?

ROGER. Ah…sure. I'll be there.

*(The bell rings ending lunch period. The **KIDS** grab their books and run wriggling their fingers in each others faces saying, "BOOGIE boogie BOOGIE boogie." **ROGER** is left alone at the table.)*

SONG - *TO MAKE THEM LIKE ME*

ROGER.

I WALK IN A ROOM
THERE'S NO ONE I KNOW
THERE'S NOTHING BUT STRANGERS AROUND ME
AND I SAY TO MYSELF
WHAT'M I GONNA DO, WHAT'M I GONNA SAY
TO MAKE THEM LIKE ME

SO I PUT ON A SMILE
AND HOLD MY HEAD HIGH
AND THOUGH I PRETEND I'M COURAGEOUS
A VOICE DEEP INSIDE SAYS
WHAT'M I GONNA DO, WHAT'M I GONNA SAY
TO MAKE THEM LIKE ME

I PRETEND THAT I'M FRIENDLY WITH KINGS AND WITH
    QUEENS
I PRETEND I'VE BEEN PLACES THAT I'VE NEVER SEEN
AND THOUGH I AM FRIGHTENED AND THOUGH IT'S A
    SHAM
I PRETEND THAT I'M ANYTHING BUT THE PERSON I AM

FROM THE WAY THAT I WALK
AND THE WAY THAT I TALK
YOU'D THINK I WAS SOMEBODY SPECIAL
BUT THE REAL ME'S INSIDE
SAYIN' WHAT'M I GONNA DO, WHAT'M I GONNA SAY
TO MAKE THEM LIKE ME

I LAUGH TILL THE TEARDROPS COME INTO MY EYES
AT STORIES I KNOW ARE AS OLD AS THE SKIES
I BLINK WITH AMAZEMENT AT SOME SILLY FACT
AND NOBODY KNOWS THAT IT'S ALL JUST AN ACT

I'D LIKE TO BELIEVE
THIS FEELING WILL LEAVE
THAT WHEN I GROW UP I CAN LAUGH AT
ALL THOSE MOMENTS I THOUGHT
WHAT'M I GONNA DO, WHAT'M I GONNA SAY
TO MAKE THEM LIKE ME

(repeat bars 46 – 55)

AT THAT VOICE DEEP INSIDE SAYIN'
WHAT'M I GONNA DO, WHAT'M I GONNA SAY
TO MAKE THEM LIKE ME

(He slowly picks up his books and exits.)

SCENE 2

(In front of curtain **SCOTT**, **JENNIFER** *and* **LAURIE** *are there wearing raincoats and holding umbrellas. Sound effect of rainfall. [SFX1 on Sound Effects CD])*

JENNIFER. Do ya think he'll come?

SCOTT. Naaah. He's chicken.

JIMMY. Here come Pam and JoAnn.

PAM. Boy, what a perfect night to go into a haunted house!

SCOTT. Where's Greg?

JOANN. I saw him coming out of his house and I think Brian's with him.

JIMMY. Here they come.

SCOTT. Hey, here comes Roger too. Hi, Rog - I knew you'd come.

ROGER. Hi. Boy, it sure is a p-p-perfect night to go into a haunted house!

SCOTT. Sure is! - I guess we're all here. Come on, follow me. I'll show you where the unlocked window is, Rog.

(They all run offstage. Curtain opens on living room of haunted house – The room is totally dark. A little light comes from outside the window. There is one window and to the right of it, one door. On the sill in front of the window is a large plastic vase. The voices of the gang come from outside.)

SCENE 3

PAM. Can you reach the window Greg?

GREG. Yeah, I can always get to it from this big rock over here. Just lean- right over to it and - push.

(Window goes up about six inches and vase in front of it falls over.)

GREG. Oh, darn. There goes that vase again!

LAURIE. Push it open a little wider, Greg, - so Roger will be able to get in.

JIMMY. And out!

(Laughter)

*(**GREG** pushes window up a little higher.)*

SCOTT. OK, Rog, - come on, we'll give you a leg up.

*(Slowly, **ROGER** appears climbing through window. Once on his feet, he begins fumbling around the dark room.)*

*(He bumps into several things. The **KIDS** call from out-side. Sound effect of rain continues.)*

LAURIE. Everything OK in there, Rog?

ROGER. Sure.

(He stumbles into chair.)

SCOTT. I thought I heard some footsteps, Rog. Did you hear 'em?

ROGER. N-N-no. That was just me - I bumped into a chair or something.

JENNIFER. Did you see anything run across the floor and go, "BOOGIE boogie BOOGIE boogie."

ROGER. N-n-no - I really can't see anything in here it's so dar-

*(Blinding light goes on in room. Man with long grey beard, **GREAT GREY GHOST**, is standing in doorway of living room - next to open window.)*

GHOST. Would you mind telling me what you're doing in MY HOUSE!

(**ROGER** *screams and runs for the window. The* **GHOST** *steps in front of it.*)

GHOST. *(cont.)* Don't you realize you are trespassing on PRIVATE PROPERTY!

ROGER. Yes. I mean n-no - I mean - Oh, please let me out!

GHOST. Maybe I'll let you out if you can give me one good reason why you are IN!

ROGER. *(trying desperately to get past him)* Oh, please … please

GHOST. Sorry, son, you're not going anywhere until you tell me what's going on here.

ROGER. *(stammering, hardly able to speak)* I just moved in next door and the kids at school said this house was haunted and I had to go into it unless I was chicken and so they lifted me through the window and…

GHOST. And what!

ROGER. *(speaking faster and faster)* And the vase fell over and then I fell over something and…

GHOST. *(dropping his scary demeanor)* Well, well… *(laughs)* I think we better have a little talk.

(*The* **GHOST** *turns and pulls down the window shade, puts the vase back, turns down light and sits down. He motions for* **ROGER** *to sit too but he remains standing.*)

GHOST. *(cont)* What's your name, son?

ROGER. *(still stammering)* Roger - Roger Brightbrill

GHOST. Well, Roger, I've been wondering what's been going on around here. See, my brother died about a year ago and left me this house. I thought I'd really like to live here…always have loved this old place. So as soon as I could rent my apartment and get my things together, I moved in. I guess the house stood here empty for a few months before I came. I didn't have to bring any furniture with me since the house was furnished and I guess nobody even realized someone had moved in. I lead a very simple life now that I'm retired - up at sunrise, to bed at sundown, don't own a car…

SONG - MY SIMPLE WAY OF LIVIN'

GHOST.

WELL, IT'S JUST MY SIMPLE WAY OF LIVIN'
UP AT DAWN AND OFF TO BED BEFORE
THE CHILL IS ON THE DOORSTEP
GIVES ME MORE PEP
THAN ANY TEENAGE BOY

YES, I LOVE MY SIMPLE WAY OF LIVIN'
NO ONE KNOWS THE WAY I SPEND MY DAYS
YOU THINK I MUST BE CRAZY
OR REALLY LAZY
BUT IT'S WHAT I ENJOY

I USED TO WORK FROM DAWN TO DUSK
I REALLY LOVED MY JOB
BUT I GOT TIRED OF THE SUBWAY, TIRED OF THE BUS
TIRED OF THE CITY MOB

NOW I'VE FOUND A SIMPLE WAY OF LIVIN'
IT'S A FACT I LIVE A LIFE OF EASE
THERE'S NO ONE THAT I'M PLEASIN'
AND THAT'S THE REASON
THIS SIMPLE WAY OF LIVIN' PLEASES ME

(This can incorporate a soft-shoe dance by **GHOST** *or the* **GHOST** *and* **ROGER***)*

GHOST. But you know, Roger, funny thing is I've always been a little scared in this house.

ROGER. *(Wide-eyed)* You have?!

GHOST. Yes - I was always hearing the sounds of footsteps creeping around outside and whispering and laughter. Why I even began to think this house might have a poltergeist!

ROGER. Wh-what's that!

GHOST. Of course, I don't believe in such things but a poltergeist is supposed to be a noisy ghost that comes into houses and knocks things over and well just makes funny things happen. Ya' see that vase over there?

(points to vase in front of window)

GHOST. *(cont.)* I must have picked that darn thing up at least a dozen times. I'd stand it up and a couple of days later, there it'd be again, on the floor. Good thing it's only plastic. Anyhow, I just couldn't figure out any other way to explain it except that maybe this house had a poltergeist - much as I didn't like the idea.

ROGER. Oh - I guess I can explain that. That vase must have fallen over every time one of the kids came in through the window.

GHOST. Oh no - I only heard sounds from the outside and sometimes the window was pushed open - and the vase knocked over, but no one's ever come in before. You are the first.

ROGER. The First!

(He leaps up.)

But they all said they'd been in here. They said they heard footsteps coming from the cellar and things running around shouting, "BOOGIE boogie BOOGIE boogie," and...

GHOST. Oh my, I think your friends have been playing a trick on you. You said you just moved here, didn't you. And I bet you thought you had to do all of this, look brave and everything, just to make them like you. Right?

ROGER. Well, you remember what it was like to be a kid...I mean it was a long time ago and everything...*(embarrassed)* Well, sorry...what I mean is when you're a kid, you just worry a lot about whether people like you... And when you go to some place new...

GHOST. Roger...I hate to tell you...It doesn't change. Why when I go some place new, where I don't know anybody, I find myself doing the silliest things.

(Music begins under end of the speech)

SONG - *TO MAKE THEM LIKE ME*

*(***GHOST*** picks up TO MAKE THEM LIKE ME at bar 23)*

GHOST.

I LAUGH TILL THE TEARDROPS COME INTO MY EYES
AT STORIES I KNOW ARE AS OLD AS THE SKIES
I BLINK WITH AMAZEMENT AT SOME SILLY FACT
AND NOBODY KNOWS THAT IT'S ALL JUST AN ACT

I USED TO BELIEVE THIS FEELING WOULD LEAVE
THAT WHEN I GREW UP I WOULD LAUGH AT
ALL THOSE MOMENTS I THOUGHT
WHAT AM I GONNA DO, WHAT AM I GONNA SAY
TO MAKE THEM LIKE ME

BUT WHAT A SURPRISE WHEN I OPEN MY EYES
AND EVERYONE'S DOIN' THE SAME THING
THE SAME VOICE INSIDE SAYIN'
WHAT'M I GONNA DO, WHAT'M I GONNA SAY
TO MAKE THEM LIKE ME

YES, GENERALS AND CZARS, TYCOONS AND STARS
ARE JUST AS AFRAID AS I AM
THE SAME VOICE INSIDE SAYS
WHAT'M I GONNA DO, WHAT'M I GONNA SAY
TO MAKE THEM LIKE ME

YES THE SAME VOICE INSIDE SAYS
WHAT'M I GONNA DO, WHAT'M I GONNA SAY
TO MAKE THEM LIKE ME

GHOST. Now, Roger, about those new friends of yours: I don't think it would hurt your standing in your new community if we…were to PLAY…A little TRICK…on THEM!

(He gets up, goes to the window and peeks out.)

GHOST. Mmm, just as I thought…Nobody there. Looks like all your friends ran off when the lights went on. But I suspect they'll be back. They'll be afraid something awful's happened to you and they better get you out of here before their parents find out what a trick they played on the new kid. Now, when they come back lets you and I have a little surprise ready for THEM.

ROGER. Ok!!

GHOST. Now, here's my idea. When I was young you know what I used to be?

ROGER. No. What?

GHOST. A sound effects man! I bet you don't even know what that is.

ROGER. No.

GHOST. Well, when we just had radio - no television - they used to have stories just like they do on TV now. But you couldn't see them - just hear. So they had to depend on sound effects to make them seem real. And boy oh boy, were they real! We could scare you right out of your boots! Like there was this slow ... squeaky ...door *(He imitates the sound.)* and then the announcer would come in and say... "Welcome ... to...Inner Sanctum..." And there was this other program that started with the sound of footsteps and a fog horn and you just knew it was night on a lonely street near the docks. Boy, you could practically feel the fog swirling up around you! I'll tell you sometimes what went on in your head was a lot scarier than what you see on a TV screen! Of course, there were some funny sound effects, too...Like Fibber McGee and Mollie's closet.

ROGER. Fibber mc-What?

GHOST. Fibber McGee...Y'see, Fibber McGee and Mollie lived at 69 Wistful Vista and in their house they had a closet where, well, whenever they couldn't figure out where to put something, they put it in that closet. And every week, yep on every show, one of'm would be lookin' for something and forget. They'd forget to be careful when they opened the closet door. "Why I think that suitcase is right in here, Mollie," Fibber would say and the folks at home would want to say, "No, Fibber, no, don't open that door!" But too late. Bam, Crash, Clatter, Bang. Oh that was wonderful! Yep. Fibber McGee and Mollie's closet. That was one of my specialties!

(He slowly folds his arms and turns to **ROGER***.)*

GHOST. Fibber McGee and Mollie's closet. Hmmm…Now that could sound pretty scary to someone standing in a darkened room…in a haunted house, couldn't it, Roger?

(Continues excitedly)

Fibber McGee's closet and squeaky doors and ghosts laughing and footsteps and screams…

(Music to the chorus of **THE HOUSE ON OLD SPOOK LANE** *plays underneath and builds to the end of the scene.)*

GHOST. Come on, Roger, come with me! The one thing I did bring along is all my old sound effects equipment! It's all down in the basement! Come on! Why, I'll show you how to make the sound of bats wings flapping, of footsteps in the fog, of Superman flying. You didn't have to SEE Superman, you just heard him and it was real as anything. And when the announcer would say, "Look! Up in the air! It's a bird! It's a Plane! It's Superman!" YOU SAW HIM!!!

(BLACK OUT)

SCENE 4

(The action takes place in the living room of the haunted house. It is dimly lit. The window shade is up and the vase is back on the floor. Voices come from outside open window.)

JENNIFER. Why'd we have to come back?

SCOTT. Are you kidding? We can't just leave him in there. Why if my parents ever found out what we put that kid up to they'd murder me!

JIMMY. I guess you're right; we'll have to go in and find him.

PAM. Where's Greg?

SCOTT. That chicken, he didn't come back!

LAURIE. No, here he comes.

SCOTT. Come on, Greg - hurry up. You go first. You know your way around inside.

GREG. I do? Oh yes, I-I do, but gee, Scott, you've been in with your sister. I mean you've already given one guided tour!

SCOTT. Aw - we didn't really get very far - you know what a chicken she is. Come on, Brian! You lead the way.

BRIAN. Me! I've never even looked through the win–I mean, well, Pam, how 'bout you?

PAM. Me! I'd never go in that house.

JENNIFER. Or me.

LAURIE. Or me

SCOTT. Hey, I thought you'd all been in there at least a dozen times, huh Greg?

GREG. Well, I got the window open a few times.

JIMMY. How 'bout you Scott, how many times you been in?

SCOTT. *(silence)* Well - come on. Give a leg up. Somebody's got to lead the way. But you'll all be right behind me, right?

GANG. Right - right - right!

(One by one they all come through the window and stand huddled together in the center of the room.)

SCOTT. *(timidly)* Roger.

JENNIFER. *(more timidly)* Roger.

LAURIE. *(more timidly)* Roger.

(strange sound [SFX2 on the sound effect CD])

SCOTT. What was that?

PAM. I'm scared.

(Sound [SFX3 on the sound effect CD])

JENNIFER. Let's get out of here.

(She starts toward the window. JIMMY reaches out and grabs her arm.)

JIMMY. No, we can't leave - we've got to find Roger!

(A scary sound [SFX4 on the sound effect CD])

PAM. Ooh –

(Followed by another sound, and another. [SFX5 on the sound effect CD]) They react.

SCOTT. Look, we all know there's no such thing as haunted, don't we?

LAURIE. Right.

JIMMY. Right.

(Another long sound. [SFX5 on the sound effect CD])

JENNIFER.. *(closing her eyes tightly)* There's no such thing as haunted - No such thing as haunted…

(opens her eyes)

ROGER !!!!

SONG - THERE'S NO SUCH THING AS HAUNTED

ALL.
> I HEARD A LOW AND MOURNFUL CRY
> FROM SOMEWHERE DOWN BELOW
> IT SOUNDS LIKE SOMEONE'S BURIED THERE
> BUT I KNOW IT CAN'T BE SO

ALL. *(cont.)*

CAUSE THERE'S NO SUCH THING
NO SUCH THING
NO SUCH THING AS BEING HAUNTED
THERE'S NO SUCH THING
NO SUCH THING
NO SUCH THING AS HAUNTED

[SFX7 on the Sound Effects CD]

I HEARD THE CREAKING OF THE FLOOR
FROM DOWN THE DARKENED HALL
I'M SURE THAT SOMEWHERE THERE'S A ROOM
FULL OF CREEPY THINGS THAT CRAWL

CAUSE THERE'S NO SUCH THING
NO SUCH THING
NO SUCH THING AS BEING HAUNTED
THERE'S NO SUCH THING
NO SUCH THING
NO SUCH THING AS HAUNTED

[SFX8 on the Sound Effects CD]

I HEAR THE TICKING OF A CLOCK
IT SOUNDS LIKE IT'S IN HERE
BUT THAT OLD CLOCK HAS LONG BEEN STOPPED
YET I HEAR IT LOUD AND CLEAR

BUT THERE'S NO SUCH THING
NO SUCH THING
NO SUCH THING AS BEING HAUNTED
THERE'S NO SUCH THING
NO SUCH THING
NO SUCH THING AS HAUNTED

[SFX9 on the Sound Effects CD]

THERE'S SOMEONE LAUGHING IN THIS ROOM
I KNOW YOU HEAR IT TOO
I NEVER BOTHERED IT BEFORE
IT MUST BE AFTER YOU!

BUT THERE'S NO SUCH THING
NO SUCH THING
NO SUCH THING AS BEING HAUNTED
THERE'S NO SUCH THING
NO SUCH THING
NO SUCH THING AS ...

(The music stops abruptly. There is a moment of silence and then a huge CRASH.)

([SFX10 on the Sound Effects CD] BAM! CLATTER! It is Fibber McGee's closet!)

ALL. ...Haunted!

(ad libbing)

I'm getting out of here! Me too!

*(The **KIDS** turn and fly out the window to the sounds of loud laugh track [SFX 11 on the Sound Effects CD]. **ROGER** and the **GHOST** enter. Their laughter blends with the sounds of the laugh track. There is a solitary boot in the middle of the floor. The **GHOST** picks it up.)*

GHOST. Well, I guess we really did scare them out of their boots, didn't we, Roger?

ROGER. *(laughing)* Yeah. You bet!

GHOST. How'd you like working all that equipment?

ROGER. *(still laughing)* It was really great!

GHOST. You'd make a pretty good sound effects man yourself!

ROGER. Thanks.

GHOST. Now listen, Roger - I'll tell you what you do. You go straight home and call those kids up, and ask them where the heck they were when you came out, fine bunch of friends! Tell them you went through the whole house and even met the Great Grey Ghost of old Spook Lane - who wasn't such a bad fellow at all. Then when you came out through the window, they were all gone. What's the idea of that?

ROGER. Yeah, what's the big idea of that!

GHOST. Then you can tell them the Great Grey Ghost of Old Spook Lane wants to meet all of them.

ROGER. Wants to meet them!?

GHOST. Sure, tell them to come over here with you tomorrow night at the same time.

ROGER. Do you think they'll come?

GHOST. They'll be scared, but they won't dare say no if it looks like you're so brave! They'll come. Get on home now. Your parents must be wondering where you are.

ROGER. OK, Mister Grey Ghost.

GHOST. Roger…My name is MUGGINS. You can call me Mr. Muggins.

ROGER. Ok, Mr. Muggins. See you tomorrow night.

SCENE 5

(Living room of haunted house, dimly lit. One by one the kids come through window, ROGER leading the way. Background music, THERE'S NO SUCH THING AS HAUNTED played very slowly.)

SCOTT. Well, Rog, w-where's the Great Grey Ghost?

(Scary sound of laughter, KIDS start for the window)

(SFX12 on the Sound Effects CD)

ROGER. *(stopping them)* Hey, come on. There's nothing to be afraid of.

JENNIFER. Yeah, that's right, there's n-no such thing as haunted.

(SFX13 on the Sound Effects CD)

JIMMY. Th-then what was that?

(SFX14 on the Sound Effects CD)

LAURIE. And that?

ROGER. Every ghost has to impress people a little the first time they meet that's just his way of showing off a little, just like humans. You do the same thing yourselves, don't you?

(to himself)

I know I do.

(SFX15 on the Sound Effects CD)

PAM. Gee, I-I wish he wouldn't worry about making such a good impression.

(Great clap of thunder followed by a sound of squeaking door [SFX16] the door at stage right opens and the GREAT GREY GHOST himself steps into the room. His face is powdered white, he has grey hair, grey beard and is dressed in a white sheet.)

(All the children but ROGER jump back.)

GHOST. Good evening my little friends. I'm so glad you accepted my invitation. Roger, will you introduce me?

ROGER. Gang, this is Mr. Mug– I mean, the GREAT GREY GHOST. Mr. Ghost this is Pam, Laurie, Scott, Jimmy.

(He introduces them all around.)

SCOTT. *(to Jimmy)* Wow, did you feel how cold his hands were - he really must be a ghost!

JIMMY. And look at his eyes…scar-ree!

JENNIFER. *(to Laurie)* Hey, look at Roger…He's not scared at all!

PAM. Boy, I wish I could get out of here!

GHOST. And now I hope you'll join me in a little party.

(He chuckles.)

GHOST. A ghostly party, that is.

*(The **GHOST** rolls out a table laden with food.)*

GHOST. It's not the kind of food you eat at home or in school but rather.

(a sinister chuckle)

My kind of food - ghostly food.

SONG - A GHOSTLY REPAST

GHOST.

HERE FOR A STARTER
(THERE'S ENOUGH FOR THE GROUP)
MY FAVORITE BROTH
EVIL EYE SOUP

NEXT, A TREAT
DEVISED BY A WIZARD
RAVIOLI STUFFED
WITH CHOPPED LIZARD GIZZARD

MY FRIEND, WHAT'S THE MATTER?
YOU LOOK A BIT PALLID
THERE'S NOTHING IN HERE
BUT SKELTON SALAD

THIS WINE TAKES AGING
YEARS IN A CRYPT
THEN POURED IN A COFFIN
AND TO ME, SHIPPED

THE CHEF WHO MADE THIS
NOW CAN RETIRE
THE TRIUMPH OF ALL
CREAM OF VAMPIRE

OR PERHAPS YOU'D PREFER
BRISKET OF SNAKE
OR MAYBE A BIT
OF WEREWOLF STEAK

THIS CRUST IS AS LIGHT
AS THE CLOUDS IN THE SKY
THE FILLINGS HARDLY THERE
IT'S PHANTOM PIE

HERE'S SOMETHING I MAKE
RIGHT IN MY TUB
JELL-O, YES, JELL-O
IN COLD BLOOD

MUMMY CAKE, MUMMY CAKE
HOW I LOVE YOU
SPRINKLED WITH TOADSTOOLS
WON'T YOU HAVE SOME, TOO?

AND NOW YOU'VE PARTAKEN
OF MY GHOSTLY REPAST
AREN'T YOU GLAD THAT YOU'VE TASTED
THESE GOODIES AT LAST?

IF YOU'VE OVER EATEN
AND FEEL A BIT CRUMMY
MAY I OFFER YOU PLEASE
SOME THUMBS FOR THE TUMMY

THUMBS OF GOBLINS
THUMBS OF GHOULS
WHEN DROPPED INTO WATER
THEY FIZZLE SO YOU'LL

THINK IT'S AS GOOD
AS THE BEST ALKA SELTZ
AND LIKE MAGIC, AWAY
THE TUMMY ACHE MELTS

OH WHAT A JOY
OH WHAT A DELIGHT
I CAN SEE THAT YOU LOVED
EVERY BITE

AND NOW IF YOU'RE ASKED
YOU MAY SAY OUTRIGHT
GHOSTLY FOOD
IS OUT - OF - SIGHT!

(During the song the **CHILDREN** *react to each thing he offers them but hardly eat a thing.)*

GHOST. Well, this certainly has been lovely, I'm so glad you could come. Thank you so much, Roger, for bringing them.

(There is a horrible sound. [SFX17] The **KIDS** *start for the window.)*

GHOST. Oh, darn, my pet ghoul. He never knows when to keep quiet. I better get down to the basement and see what he wants.

*(***KIDS** *rush to the window and scramble out.* **ROGER** *turns and smiles at the* **GHOST**. **GHOST** *comes over and puts his arm around him, taking off his white sheet.)*

GHOST. Now listen, young man, before you go I want you to promise me one thing. That you'll be real careful from now on - I mean for now and forever - about what you do just to make someone like you. OK?

ROGER. *(He looks at his feet and chuckles.)* OK, Mr. Muggins. I'll remember that. For now and forever.

(He climbs through the window looking back to give the **GHOST** *one last wave.)*

SCENE 6

*(Cafeteria the next day. Two tables get pushed together as usual by the **KIDS**. They put their trays down and start eating, discussing **ROGER**'s bravery.)*

SCOTT. Wow! Did you see Roger when those screams started? He didn't even blink an eye!

JENNIFER. *(dreamily)* Yeah. He sure is brave.

JIMMY. I still can't believe I really met a ghost!

PAM. And shook hands with him!

LAURIE. Eeooo - those cold clammy hands!

GREG. And how 'bout that food?

JO ANN. Yeah, Greg, This stuff even tastes good after that!

BRIAN. Jell-o in cold blood - I don't think I'll ever eat Jell-o again!

SCOTT. Hey, you guys, did any one save a seat for Roger?

*(**ROGER** enters nonchalantly.)*

ROGER. Hi, Gang.

GANG. *(admiringly)* Hi, Roger.

JENNIFER. Will you sit with us, Roger?

BRIAN. Over here!

JO ANN. No, sit over here!

*(**ROGER** sits down.)*

SCOTT. Wow, that was really something last night Rog, old pal!

JENNIFER. *(dreamily)* Yeah, you didn't let that old ghost worry you a bit.

ROGER. Well. I guess it's best to keep an open mind about people and ghosts until you get to know them. You might like them.

SCOTT. Yeah.

JIMMY. Yeah!

(Curtain.)

SCENE 7

*(In front of curtain. There is a doorway marked 17 IVY ROAD. **ROGER** is knocking on **THE GHOST**'s front door. No one answers. There is the sound of a car pulling up and then a voice.)*

VOICE. Hey, sonny, you're not going to get any answer at that door. Old fella that lived there died about a year ago.

ROGER. Oh no sir, you must be wrong. I saw him just yesterday.

VOICE. Well, I'm in charge of keepin' a look out on the place, till they get things straightened out. They're having a hard time finding any next of kin. But I can assure you, the place has been empty since last November. Now you run on home.

*(The car pulls away. **ROGER** stands there for a moment unsure of what to do. He starts to knock again. Then stops, shakes his head, and slowly starts walking towards home.)*

END

*(Curtain call music: **TO MAKE THEM LIKE ME** (reprise))*

OTHER TITLES AVAILABLE FROM BAKER'S PLAYS

HARRIET AND WALT

Book and Lyrics by Jennifer Kirkeby
Music by Shirley Mier
Based on the Book by Nancy Carlson

TYA, Children's Theatre / 4m, 9f / Simple Set

Pre-teen Harriet always gets stuck with her little brother Walt tagging along everywhere she goes. The last thing she wants is an accident prone little brother interfering with her and her friends' preparations for the Winter Carnival. When Walt almost gets hurt, Harriet realizes how much he means to her and stands up to her friend George, who criticized her kid brother.

Based on the classic childrens' book by Nancy Carlson, *Harriet and Walt,* this story teaches an important lesson about sibling rivalry.